THE GIRL WITH GREEN EYES

Greg works at the Shepton Hotel in New York. Opposite the hotel there is a coffee shop, and Greg goes there for a coffee every day after work. Every day he sees a girl there with beautiful green eyes. One day, Greg sits next to the girl. She tells him her name is Cassie, and she asks him for help.

Cassie tells Greg that she is an artist. She says her stepfather has her sketch books, and Cassie wants them back. She also says her stepfather is staying at the Shepton Hotel, so Greg agrees to help.

Greg is very happy when he gets the sketch books and gives them to Cassie. Cassie is very happy, too.

But then Greg meets his friend Mike. Mike tells Greg that he's in trouble. The police want to talk to him and are waiting at his apartment.

What is wrong? Why do the police want to talk to Greg?

OXFORD BOOKWORMS LIBRARY

Crime & Mystery

The Girl with Green Eyes

Starter (250 headwords)

JOHN ESCOTT

The Girl
with Green Eyes

Illustrated by
Dylan Gibson

OXFORD UNIVERSITY PRESS

OXFORD
UNIVERSITY PRESS

Great Clarendon Street, Oxford, OX2 6DP, United Kingdom

Oxford University Press is a department of the University of Oxford.
It furthers the University's objective of excellence in research, scholarship,
and education by publishing worldwide. Oxford is a registered trade
mark of Oxford University Press in the UK and in certain other countries

This simplified edition © Oxford University Press 2012

The moral rights of the author have been asserted

First published in Oxford Bookworms 2012

10 9 8 7 6 5 4 3 2 1

ISBN: 978 0 19 479434 3   Reader
ISBN: 978 0 19 479433 6   Audio CD Pack

Printed in China

Word count (main text): 1550

For more information on the Oxford Bookworms Library,
visit www.oup.com/elt/bookworms

CONTENTS

The Girl
with Green Eyes

Greg is a porter at the Shepton Hotel in New York. After work, he always goes for a coffee across the street. A girl is sitting in the coffee shop, near the window.

'It's her again!' thinks Greg. 'She's here every afternoon. I'm going to say hello.'

Greg goes into the coffee shop and gets a coffee. Then he goes across to the girl's table.

'Hi!' he says. 'I'm Greg. Can I sit with you?'

'OK,' she says. 'I'm Cassie.'

'I come here for a coffee every day after work,' says Greg. 'I'm a porter at the Shepton Hotel.' He smiles. 'You have beautiful green eyes.'

'Have I?' she says. She doesn't smile.

'Is something wrong, Cassie?' he asks. 'You don't look very happy.'

'It – it's nothing,' she says.

'Tell me,' says Greg. 'Maybe I can help?'

'Well . . .' she begins.

'Go on,' says Greg.

'My stepfather is staying at the Shepton Hotel,' she says. 'He has my sketch books. I'm an artist. When I ask him to give them to me he says, "No. I want you to come back home to Boston." But I don't want to go back to Boston. He's not nice.'

'How long is he going to be at the hotel?' asks Greg.

'Two more days,' says Cassie. 'He's in room 724.'

'Maybe I can get the sketch books for you,' says Greg. 'Maybe I can get into his room.'

'Can you?' she says.

'Meet me here tomorrow afternoon at 4.30,' says Greg.

'OK, thank you!' says Cassie. 'Thank you very much.' She looks at her watch. 'I've got to go now. See you tomorrow.'

When Cassie gets back to her hotel room, she makes a telephone call.

'Hello,' she says. 'It's me. It's OK, the boy's going to do it . . . Yes, I'm going to get them from him tomorrow afternoon . . . OK, I can meet you there the morning after, at 10am. Don't forget to bring the money – two thousand dollars.'

Next morning, Greg arrives at work early. He goes to find room 724.

'I have to wait for Cassie's stepfather to go out,' he thinks. 'I don't know his name, but it doesn't matter.'

Greg watches the door of room 724. He sees the girl come to clean the rooms.

Some minutes later, a man comes out of room 724.

'That must be Cassie's stepfather!' thinks Greg.

He waits for the man to leave, and for the cleaning girl to go into room 724.

'I need to look in the room,' he thinks.

Greg waits for the girl to leave the bedroom, then he goes into the room and begins to look for the sketch books.

'I must be quick,' he thinks. 'Where are they?'

Suddenly, Greg sees the sketch books by the bed.

'Got them!' he thinks. He begins to look at the pictures. 'Wow! Cassie is a great artist! These are good!'

Greg is leaving the room when he hears the cleaning girl call out to him.

'Hey!' she says. 'What are you doing? Come back!'

Greg does not stop.

Greg finishes work that afternoon and leaves the hotel through a door in the next street. When he gets near the front of the hotel, he sees the man from room 724.

'That's him again!' thinks Greg. 'That's Cassie's stepfather.'

Greg waits for the man to go into the hotel, then he goes to the coffee shop.

Cassie is at the same table in the coffee shop.

Greg gets a coffee and goes to sit with her.

'I have them,' he says, and he puts the sketch books on the table.

'That's great!' says Cassie. 'How can I thank you, Greg?'

'You can meet me later,' he says. 'After I go home and change out of my porter's uniform.'

'I'm sorry, Greg,' says Cassie. 'I can't tonight. Maybe tomorrow night.'

'OK,' says Greg. 'Tomorrow night. We can get something to eat, first.'

'Yes, OK,' says Cassie. 'I have to go now, but meet me here tomorrow evening at six o'clock.'

Cassie gets up, ready to leave.

'Don't forget your key,' says Greg.

'Oh – er – thanks,' says Cassie. She takes it from him quickly. 'See you tomorrow.'

Greg is finishing his coffee when he sees his friend, Mike.

'You're in trouble, Greg,' says Mike. 'Jake Russo's sketch books are not in his room – room 724. And there are CCTV pictures of you coming from that room.'

'Wh – who is Jake Russo?' asks Greg. Suddenly he's not feeling very well.

'An artist,' says Mike. 'His pictures sell for thousands of dollars. And his sketch books sell for thousands, too.'

'Do you have them?' asks Mike.

'No – er – a girl has them,' says Greg.

'What girl?' asks Mike.

'A girl with green eyes,' says Greg. And he tells Mike about Cassie and her stepfather.

'But it's not true!' says Mike, when Greg finishes speaking. 'Jake Russo doesn't have a wife or a stepdaughter. You have to find that girl and get the sketch books, Greg. And you have to do it before the police find you!'

Greg walks home to his one-room apartment.

'How am I going to find her?' he thinks. 'She has Jake Russo's sketch books now, so she's not going to meet me again. Is she going to sell them for a lot of money?'

There is a police car in the street, next to Greg's apartment.

'Oh, no!' he thinks. 'They're waiting for me. I can't get into my apartment now.'

That night, Greg sleeps on a train in the subway. But early the next morning . . .

'Hey, you!' says a man. He's the subway cleaner. 'Get up! You can't sleep here all day!'

'Sorry,' says Greg.

People are arriving to get their trains now. One of them stops and looks at a photograph in his newspaper – and then at Greg.

'It's him,' thinks the man. 'It's the young man in the newspaper photograph. The police are looking for him.'

Suddenly, Greg sees the man looking at him. And he sees his picture on the front of the man's newspaper.

'I have to get out of here quickly!' he thinks.

The man with the newspaper finds a policeman.
  'It's him!' he tells the policeman. 'The hotel porter!'
  'Hey, you!' the policeman calls to Greg.

Greg runs.
  'Stop!' calls the policeman.
Greg doesn't stop.

'I have to get out of this uniform,' thinks Greg. 'People know I'm the porter. Maybe Mike can give me something different to wear.'

When he gets to Mike's apartment, Mike opens the door. 'I need something to wear,' Greg tells him. 'I can't go back to my apartment. My picture's in the newspaper, and —'

'Yes, I know,' says Mike. 'It's OK. Come in.'

'Where's the girl?' asks Mike. 'Do you know?'

'No,' says Greg.

'What can you remember about her?' says Mike. 'There must be something to help you find her.'

'Yes!' Greg says, suddenly. 'Her key! A key to a room in the Dolphin Hotel! It's a small, cheap hotel near 42nd Street. She must be staying there. What's the time?'

'Nearly nine o'clock,' says Mike.

'Maybe she's there now,' says Greg. 'I have to go! Thanks, Mike.'

19

Twenty minutes later, Greg is near the Dolphin Hotel.

'Am I too late?' he thinks.

Suddenly, Greg sees Cassie come out of the hotel.

'Cassie!' he calls. 'Wait! I have to talk to you!'

Cassie sees him, but she doesn't stop. There is a car waiting for her. She says something to the driver and gets into it quickly.

'Oh, no!' says Greg.

'Pier 83,' says an old man in the street.

Greg looks at him. 'What?'

'The girl is going to Pier 83, West 42nd Street, for the Circle Line boat,' says the old man.

Greg smiles. 'Thanks!' he says. And he begins to run.

Greg runs all the way to Pier 83. People are getting on to the boat, and he gets a ticket.

On the boat, Greg looks for Cassie. But a woman with a newspaper is looking at him.

'It's the young man in the picture!' she tells the man with her. 'Call the police, Eddie.'

The man gets his phone and calls the police.

Some time later, Greg sees Cassie. She is talking to a man. But Greg does not see two policemen get on the boat.

They quickly find Greg. 'Where are Jake Russo's sketch books?' the first policeman asks him.

'I don't have them!' says Greg. 'You don't want me! You want her! She has the sketch books.'

'Hey, look! He's right,' says the second policeman.

The two policemen move quickly to Cassie and the man.

'I don't understand,' says Cassie. 'How . . . ?'

'The two of you are coming with us,' says one of the policemen. 'You're in trouble.'

Later, Greg and a policeman take the sketch books back to the hotel. Jake Russo is very happy to see them again.

'I'm sorry, Mr Russo,' says Greg, and tells him everything.

'It's OK,' says the artist, smiling. 'But stay away from girls with beautiful green eyes!'

GLOSSARY

apartment a room or group of rooms where you can live

artist someone who paints, draws, or makes pictures

boat a small ship

clean *(v)* make something free from dirt

coffee a hot drink

dollars money used in America ($)

hotel a building where you can pay to stay in a room

key you use this to lock and unlock a door

newspaper where you can read about the things happening every day

pier a wall from the land into the sea where people get on and off boats

police the men and women who catch criminals

porter a man who carries your bags at a hotel

sell *(v)* give someone something and get money for it

sketch *(n)* a quick drawing of something

stepfather a man who is not your father but who marries your mother

subway American word for underground railway

trouble something which causes a problem

uniform special clothes for a job

The Girl with Green Eyes

ACTIVITIES

Before Reading

1 Look at the front cover of the book and answer these questions.

1 Where do you think the story happens?

   a □ Japan

   b □ America

   c □ Spain

   d □ Brazil

2 What do you think the story is about?

   a □ children

   b □ old people

   c □ young people

   d □ animals

2 Read the back cover of the book and answer these questions.

1 Where does Greg work?

2 What does Cassie tell Greg?

3 Do you think Greg is good or bad? Why?

4 Do you think Cassie is good or bad? Why?

While Reading

1 Read pages 1 – 4 and answer these questions.

1 What does Greg always do after work?
2 Who is sitting at a table near the window?
3 What does she want?
4 Who has got them?
5 Greg tells Cassie to meet him again. When?

2 Read pages 5 – 8 and answer these questions.

1 Cassie goes back to her hotel room. What does she do next?
2 How much money does she want?
3 Which room does Greg watch?
4 Who goes into the room before Greg?
5 What does Greg find in the room?

3 Read pages 9 – 12. Who says or thinks these words?

1 'That's him again!'
2 'Meet me here tomorrow evening at six o'clock.'
3 'Don't forget your key.'
4 'You're in trouble, Greg.'
5 'Who is Jake Russo?'

4 Read pages 13 – 16. Are these sentences true (T) or false (F)?

	T	F
1 Greg gets a train home to his apartment.	☐	☐
2 There is a police car in the street, next to Greg's apartment.	☐	☐
3 Greg sleeps on a train.	☐	☐
4 A man sees Greg's picture on the TV.	☐	☐
5 Greg sees the man looking at him.	☐	☐

5 Read pages 17 – 20 and answer these questions.

1 What does the man with the newspaper do?
2 Why does Greg go to Mike's apartment?
3 What does Greg remember about his meeting with Cassie?
4 Where is the Dolphin Hotel?
5 What is waiting for Cassie near the hotel?

6 Before you read pages 21 – 24, can you guess what happens?

	Yes	No
1 Greg follows Cassie's car in a different car.	☐	☐
2 Somebody tells Greg where Cassie is going.	☐	☐
3 The police find Cassie before Greg finds her.	☐	☐
4 Cassie sells the sketch books before Greg finds her.	☐	☐
5 Greg gives the sketch books back to Jake Russo.	☐	☐

Now read pages 21 – 24 to find out the answers.

After Reading

1 Put these sentences in the right order.

a ☐ Cassie tells Greg about the sketch books.

b ☐ Mike tells Greg, 'You're in trouble.'

c ☐ Greg sleeps on a train in the subway.

d ☐ Greg sees the girl in the coffee shop.

e ☐ A woman on the boat sees Greg's picture in the newspaper.

f ☐ Greg tells Jake Russo everything.

g ☐ Greg watches the door of room 724.

h ☐ Greg goes to Mike's apartment.

i ☐ The man with the newspaper in the subway finds a policeman.

j ☐ Greg runs all the way to Pier 83.

k ☐ Greg waits for the cleaning girl to leave the bedroom.

l ☐ Cassie gets back to her hotel room and makes a phone call.

m ☐ Greg gives Cassie the sketch books.

2 Use these words to join the sentences together.

or   through   then   to   at

1 Greg is a porter. The Shepton Hotel in New York.
2 Greg leaves the hotel. A door in the next street.
3 Greg gets a cup of coffee. He goes to sit with Cassie.
4 Jake Russo doesn't have a wife. A stepdaughter.
5 Greg walks home. His one-room apartment.

3 Look at each picture and answer the questions.

Where are Greg and Cassie?
Why is Cassie unhappy?

What is Greg looking for?
Why? Does he find them?

Why can't Greg go back to his
apartment? What does he do?

What is Cassie doing? Why?
What happens next?

ABOUT THE AUTHOR

John Escott worked in business before becoming a writer.
He has written many books for readers of all ages, but
enjoys writing crime and mystery thrillers most of all. He
was born in Somerset, in the west of England, but now lives
in Bournemouth, on the south coast.

He has written or retold more than twenty popular stories for
the Oxford Bookworms Library. His original stories include
Dead Man's Money (Starter), *Star Reporter* (Starter),
Girl on a Motorcycle (Starter), *Goodbye, Mr Hollywood*
(Stage 1), and *Sister Love and Other Crime Stories* (Stage 1).

OXFORD BOOKWORMS LIBRARY

Classics • Crime & Mystery • Factfiles • Fantasy & Horror
Human Interest • Playscripts • Thriller & Adventure
True Stories • World Stories

The OXFORD BOOKWORMS LIBRARY provides enjoyable reading in English, with a wide range of classic and modern fiction, non-fiction, and plays. It includes original and adapted texts in seven carefully graded language stages, which take learners from beginner to advanced level. An overview is given on the next pages.

All Stage 1 titles are available as audio recordings, as well as over eighty other titles from Starter to Stage 6. All Starters and many titles at Stages 1 to 4 are specially recommended for younger learners. Every Bookworm is illustrated, and Starters and Factfiles have full-colour illustrations.

The OXFORD BOOKWORMS LIBRARY also offers extensive support. Each book contains an introduction to the story, notes about the author, a glossary, and activities. Additional resources include tests and worksheets, and answers for these and for the activities in the books. There is advice on running a class library, using audio recordings, and the many ways of using Oxford Bookworms in reading programmes. Resource materials are available on the website <www.oup.com/bookworms>.

The *Oxford Bookworms Collection* is a series for advanced learners. It consists of volumes of short stories by well-known authors, both classic and modern. Texts are not abridged or adapted in any way, but carefully selected to be accessible to the advanced student.

You can find details and a full list of titles in the *Oxford Bookworms Library Catalogue* and *Oxford English Language Teaching Catalogues*, and on the website <www.oup.com/bookworms>.

THE OXFORD BOOKWORMS LIBRARY
GRADING AND SAMPLE EXTRACTS

STARTER • 250 HEADWORDS

present simple – present continuous – imperative –
can/cannot, must – going to (future) – simple gerunds ...

Her phone is ringing – but where is it?

Sally gets out of bed and looks in her bag. No phone.
She looks under the bed. No phone. Then she looks behind
the door. There is her phone. Sally picks up her phone and
answers it. *Sally's Phone*

STAGE 1 • 400 HEADWORDS

... past simple – coordination with *and, but, or* –
subordination with *before, after, when, because, so* ...

I knew him in Persia. He was a famous builder and I
worked with him there. For a time I was his friend, but
not for long. When he came to Paris, I came after him –
I wanted to watch him. He was a very clever, very
dangerous man. *The Phantom of the Opera*

STAGE 2 • 700 HEADWORDS

... present perfect – *will* (future) – *(don't) have to, must not, could* –
comparison of adjectives – simple *if* clauses – past continuous –
tag questions – *ask/tell* + infinitive ...

While I was writing these words in my diary, I decided
what to do. I must try to escape. I shall try to get down the
wall outside. The window is high above the ground, but
I have to try. I shall take some of the gold with me – if I
escape, perhaps it will be helpful later. *Dracula*

... should, may – present perfect continuous – *used to* – past perfect – causative – relative clauses – indirect statements ...

Of course, it was most important that no one should see Colin, Mary, or Dickon entering the secret garden. So Colin gave orders to the gardeners that they must all keep away from that part of the garden in future. **The Secret Garden**

STAGE 4 • 1400 HEADWORDS

... past perfect continuous – passive (simple forms) – *would* conditional clauses – indirect questions – relatives with *where/when* – gerunds after prepositions/phrases ...

I was glad. Now Hyde could not show his face to the world again. If he did, every honest man in London would be proud to report him to the police. **Dr Jekyll and Mr Hyde**

STAGE 5 • 1800 HEADWORDS

... future continuous – future perfect – passive (modals, continuous forms) – *would have* conditional clauses – modals + perfect infinitive ...

If he had spoken Estella's name, I would have hit him. I was so angry with him, and so depressed about my future, that I could not eat the breakfast. Instead I went straight to the old house. **Great Expectations**

STAGE 6 • 2500 HEADWORDS

... passive (infinitives, gerunds) – advanced modal meanings – clauses of concession, condition

When I stepped up to the piano, I was confident. It was as if I knew that the prodigy side of me really did exist. And when I started to play, I was so caught up in how lovely I looked that I didn't worry how I would sound. **The Joy Luck Club**

Dead Man's Money

JOHN ESCOTT

When Cal Dexter rents one of the Blue Lake Cabins, he finds
$3000 – under the floor! He doesn't know it, but it is the money
from a bank robbery. A dead man's money.

'Do I take it to the police?' he thinks.

But three more people want the money, and two of them are
dangerous.

Sally's Phone

CHRISTINE LINDOP

Sally is always running – and she has her phone with her all the
time: at home, on the train, at work, at lunchtime, and at the shops.

But then one afternoon suddenly she has a different phone . . .
and it changes her life.

Red Roses

CHRISTINE LINDOP

'Who is the man with the roses in his hand?' thinks Anna. 'I want to meet him.'

'Who is the girl with the guitar?' thinks Will. 'I like her. I want to meet her.'

But they do not meet.

'There are lots of men!' says Anna's friend Vicki, but Anna cannot forget Will. And then one rainy day . . .

Taxi of Terror

PHILLIP BURROWS AND MARK FOSTER

'How does it work?' Jack asks when he opens his present – a mobile phone. Later that night, Jack is a prisoner in a taxi in the empty streets of the dark city. He now tries his mobile phone for the first time. Can it save his life?

BOOKWORMS · THRILLER & ADVENTURE · STAGE 1

The President's Murderer

JENNIFER BASSETT

The President is dead!

A man is running in the night. He is afraid and needs to rest. But there are people behind him – people with lights, and dogs, and guns.

A man is standing in front of a desk. His boss is very angry, and the man is tired and needs to sleep. But first he must find the other man, and bring him back – dead or alive.

Two men: the hunter and the hunted. Which will win and which will lose?

Long live the President!

BOOKWORMS · CRIME & MYSTERY · STAGE 1

Love or Money?

ROWENA AKINYEMI

It is Molly Clarkson's fiftieth birthday. She is having a party. She is rich, but she is having a small party – only four people. Four people, however, who all need the same thing: they need her money. She will not give them the money, so they are waiting for her to die. And there are other people who are also waiting for her to die.

But one person can't wait. And so, on her fiftieth birthday, Molly Clarkson is going to die.